Dear Parent:
Your child's love of reading starts here!

Every child learns to read in a different way and at his or her own speed. Some go back and forth between reading levels and read favorite books again and again. Others read through each level in order. You can help your young reader improve and become more confident by encouraging his or her own interests and abilities. From books your child reads with you to the first books he or she reads alone, there are I Can Read Books for every stage of reading:

SHARED READING
Basic language, word repetition, and whimsical illustrations, ideal for sharing with your emergent reader

BEGINNING READING
Short sentences, familiar words, and simple concepts for children eager to read on their own

READING WITH HELP
Engaging stories, longer sentences, and language play for developing readers

READING ALONE
Complex plots, challenging vocabulary, and high-interest topics for the independent reader

ADVANCED READING
Short paragraphs, chapters, and exciting themes for the perfect bridge to chapter books

I Can Read Books have introduced children to the joy of reading since 1957. Featuring award-winning authors and illustrators and a fabulous cast of beloved characters, I Can Read Books set the standard for beginning readers.

A lifetime of discovery begins with the magical words "I Can Read!"

Visit www.icanread.com for information
on enriching your child's reading experience.

I Can Read Book® is a trademark of HarperCollins Publishers.

The Berenstain Bears: Gone Fishin'
Copyright ©2014 by Berenstain Publishing, Inc.
All rights reserved. Printed in the United States of America.
No part of this book may be used or reproduced in any manner whatsoever without written permission except in the case of brief quotations embodied in critical articles and reviews. For information address HarperCollins Children's Books, a division of HarperCollins Publishers, 195 Broadway, New York, NY 10007.
www.icanread.com
Library of Congress catalog card number: 2013951082
ISBN 978-0-06-207560-4 (trade bdg.)—ISBN 978-0-06-207559-8 (pbk.)

14 15 16 17 18   PC/WOR   10 9 8 7 6 5 4 3 2   ❖   First Edition

The Berenstain Bears®

GONE FISHIN'!

by Mike Berenstain
From the characters created by Stan and Jan Berenstain

HARPER
An Imprint of HarperCollinsPublishers

Papa Bear loved to fish.

He fished with a fancy rod

and reel.

He caught lots of big fish.

Brother, Sister, and Honey

loved to fish, too.

They fished with plain poles and lines.

They caught lots of little fish.

One day, the cubs went fishing.

Papa saw them going.

"I will go with you," he said.

"I will show you how to catch

big fish!"

They went down to the pond.

Papa fished with his fancy

rod and reel.

Brother, Sister, and Honey fished

with their plain poles and lines.

"I have a bite!" called Papa.

His rod bent over.

"It must be a big one!" he said.

He pulled in his line.

It was hard to do.

But it turned out to be just
an old boot.

"We have bites, too!" called
Brother, Sister, and Honey.
They pulled in their lines.

They caught three nice little fish.

"Hmm!" said Papa.

He fished some more.

He got another bite.

His rod bent over again.

He pulled in his line.

He pulled really hard.

But all he caught
was an old tire.

Brother, Sister, and Honey
caught more fish.
They caught lots of
nice little fish.

"Grrr!" said Papa.

He grabbed his rod.

He threw out his line . . . *far*!

"I have another bite!"

called Papa. "It is a big one!"

He tried to pull in his line.

But he could not pull it in.

Papa got yanked into the water.

He made a big splash!

"Look!" said the cubs.

"Your splash scared a

big fish out of the water."

Papa and the cubs took

the big fish home to Mama.

"Look what Papa caught!"

said the cubs.

The cubs were proud of their fisherman papa!